HAMMERIN'
AT HISTORY

A MAGIC LOCKER ADVENTURE

PETE BIRLE

Hammerin' at History
A Magic Locker Adventure

Copyright © 2015

Published by Scobre Educational

Written by Pete Birle

Printed in the United States of America.

Scobre Educational
2255 Calle Clara
La Jolla, CA 92037

Scobre Operations & Administration
42982 Osgood Road
Fremont, CA 94539

www.scobre.com
info@scobre.com

Scobre Educational publications may be purchased for
educational, business, or sales promotional use.

Cover and layout design by Jana Ramsay
Copyedited by Renae Reed

ISBN: 978-1-62920-119-1 (Soft Cover)
ISBN: 978-1-62920-118-4 (Library Bound)
ISBN: 978-1-62920-117-7 (eBook)

TABLE OF CONTENTS

1
DOWN SOUTH

"We're in a ballpark," said Juanito atop the steps, his head swinging from side to side.

"Well, it sure isn't Jamie's garage," said MJ with concern in his voice. "I just knew it. We're never going to get back home."

Despite fulfilling their task, helping Mike Eruzione score the winning goal for the U.S. men's hockey team against the Soviet Union in the 1980 Olympics, the magic locker had not returned the children home—as expected.

"Don't worry, MJ," said Jamie.

"Yeah," said Juanito. "This could turn out to be just as awesome as our last trip. You *did* think that was cool, didn't you?"

"It was *way* cool," said MJ. "I'm just worried about my mom coming down on me for not being home."

"She doesn't even know you left," said Jamie. "Remember, time hasn't moved."

But something had indeed gone wrong. Or more accurately, something *else* had gone wrong . . . with an athlete from the past.

"I guess it means there's more work for us to do before we *can* go home," said MJ.

Jamie gave her friend a comforting pat on the back.

"Since we're here, we might as well find where— and when—we are," said Jamie. As she turned to close the door of the locker, she noticed that on the floor sat three baseball mitts and three pairs of spikes.

"Should we bring those with us?" asked MJ.

"Why not?" answered Juanito. "While we're here—

wherever that is—we might as well play some ball."

"I'm guessing we're here *to* play ball," said Jamie.

"We're in some place called 'Mo-byle,'" said Juanito, who had walked down the hallway a bit and now stood in front of a closed door. On it was a sign that said "Manager's Office, Mobile Black Bears."

"It's pronounced 'Mo-beel,' and it's in Alabama," said the Coach, who just at that moment appeared from inside the locker.

"A lot of great baseball players came from Mobile," he continued, "like Satchel Paige, Willie McCovey, Ozzie Smith, and Hank Aaron."

"You think they played here?" asked Juanito, pointing to the sign he was now standing under that said "Welcome to Hartwell Field."

"Maybe one of them is playing here *today*," said the Coach.

"Is that why we traveled here instead of going back home?" asked Jamie excitedly.

But before she got an answer, the Coach disappeared

down the hallway and into thin air.

CRACK!

The sound of a bat hitting a ball interrupted their conversation.

The three kids turned, climbed all the way up the steps, and walked out onto the field. There, they saw a baseball team in the middle of its pre-game practice.

"We've gone back in time again," said Jamie.

"How can you be sure?" asked Juanito.

"*That's* how," said Jamie, pointing to the field.

While some players were hitting, others were fielding grounders and fly balls. Pitchers and catchers were warming up off to the side. A few reserves were running sprints along the outfield wall. Coaches were talking amongst themselves near the first-base dugout.

While none of that seemed out of the ordinary, the following observation did. . . .

Every one of them was black.

2
THE PRODIGY

"You're the only white person here," MJ said to Jamie, scanning Hartwell Field.

"I've never seen anything like this," Juanito replied, his eyes darting all over the diamond.

"We must have traveled back to when black players had their own league," said Jamie. "They called it the Negro League."

"Do you think any of the guys from Mobile that the Coach mentioned are down there?" asked MJ.

"Maybe," said Jamie.

"Well, whoever they are, they're pretty good," said Juanito, "especially that guy at shortstop."

The children watched as a skinny kid, who seemed much younger than the rest of his teammates, fielded grounders at short. Both his feet and his release were lightning fast, and he was skilled at turning the double play.

A few minutes later, the time travelers heard one of the coaches shout, "Batting practice!"

A few of the players jogged in toward home. The kids watched as the young shortstop grabbed a bat and slowly walked to the plate.

"Man, he looks like he'd rather take a nap than step into the batter's box," said Juanito.

"Yeah, he looks like he doesn't even want to bat," said MJ.

The young hitter calmly dug in on the right side of the plate and glanced out at the pitcher. He looked lazy.

He was anything but lazy, though. He promptly swung at the first pitch he saw, driving it into the gap in left-center.

"Way to go, Henry!" yelled one of the coaches.

"That's the way to stroke it, Henry," shouted one of his teammates.

"Did you hear that?" said MJ. "They called him Henry."

"Yeah," said Juanito. "That's got to be Hank Aaron!"

"I bet you're right," said Jamie, "only I didn't know he was a shortstop."

"Best shortstop in the Mobile City Recreation League," said a deep voice.

Startled, the children turned to see not the Coach but a distinguished looking, well-dressed black man, with a felt hat sitting on his head. He was approaching them from behind.

"Now, what are you three doing in here?" asked the man, looking especially at Jamie. She did stand out. "The game isn't starting for another two hours."

"Sorry, mister," said Jamie, thinking quickly. "We're not from around here, and we kind of just wandered in to see who was playing."

"I see you got your gear," said the man. "Are you ballplayers?"

"Yup. We sure are," answered Juanito. "But we're not as good as those guys down there."

"Well, don't be bothered about that, son," said the man. "Not many folks are."

"Hey, mister," said MJ. "Is that really Hank Aaron at bat?"

"Sure is," said the man. "Can you believe he's only 17 years old and still in high school?"

The children all turned to stare at each other. Their eyes met as they realized how far back in time they had gone in the locker.

"How do you kids know Henry Aaron?" asked the man.

"Everybody knows Hank Aaron," said MJ rather matter-of-factly. "He was the best."

Both Jamie and Juanito shot MJ a look.

"Was?" asked the man. "Son, he's just starting out."

"I meant *is*," MJ corrected quickly.

The man chuckled.

"You know him?" asked Jamie.

"I sure do," said the man. "I'm Herbert Aaron, his father."

The children smiled. They could hardly believe they were standing there talking to Hank Aaron's dad.

"Did you teach him to play?" asked Juanito.

"I wish I could take credit for that," said Herbert Aaron. "No, Henry had a gift, from the first time he picked up a baseball. Even if he does look like he's asleep half the time."

"He's batting cross-handed, though," said Juanito.

"I know," said Hank's dad. "It's something, him being able to hit with his hands the wrong way."

Hank's dad left, and Jamie turned to her friends.

"I think I know why we're here," she said. "It's to help Hank Aaron, the greatest home run hitter of all time, break his habit of batting cross-handed."

"Hey, what are you three doing?"

The kids turned to see a police officer coming toward them.

"You're not supposed to be in here yet."

"We can't leave," whispered MJ to his pals. "We'll have to sneak back in then, and they'll be watching us."

"What should we do?" asked Jamie, for once uncertain of an answer.

"Run!" yelled Juanito, who was, as usual, not afraid to act.

The kids took off, the policeman hot on their tail.

"We've got—to try to lose him—inside the ballpark," said Jamie, in full stride. "We're here to help—Hank Aaron!"

The kids made their way back into the hallway where they had left the locker. The cop was right behind them.

"You three, stop right there!" he yelled.

With nowhere to go, the children had no choice but to climb back into the locker and close the door. . . .

3
STAR-CROSSED

The first thing the children noticed upon opening the door of the locker was that, once again, they had not returned home.

The second thing they noticed was that wherever they were now, it wasn't Mobile, Alabama.

A third thing: They were once again inside what looked like a ballpark.

"Where are we now?" asked MJ.

"Beats me," said Jamie. "But I bet Hank Aaron is here. It's our job to find him and get him to hold his hands the right way on the bat."

"Why are you so sure that's what we're supposed to do?" asked Juanito. "He seemed to hit pretty good cross-handed."

"That's *got* to be the reason," said Jamie. "Look, we still have the mitts and cleats. We *need* to find Hank Aaron and play some baseball with him. If he didn't need us, we'd be back in the garage already."

At that point, the three kids heard voices coming from the doorway of the clubhouse. They realized they were only a few feet away, the locker having landed in the hallway outside. They could easily be spotted, so they ducked behind it.

"He arrives on the train today from Mobile," said a black man, who had just entered the hallway. He was dressed in a baseball uniform that said "Clowns" across the jersey.

"For $200 a month, he better be good," said a white man, who was dressed in a business suit. "I expect him to spend very little time in the Negro Leagues before moving on to the bigs."

"Don't worry, Mr. Pollock," said the first man. "Henry Aaron will prove to be money well spent, even before the 1952 season is over. The major league teams will let you know just how much Erin is worth."

The men started to walk away, thankfully in the opposite direction of the children. Once they were gone, the three friends pushed the locker down the hallway and out of view, past bathrooms marked for "white" and "colored."

"What do those signs mean?" asked Juanito.

"Back in 1952, the South was segregated," said the Coach, who had just arrived. "Blacks and whites didn't use the same restrooms or drink from the same water fountains. Things were separate, and they weren't equal. African Americans were wrongly treated like second-class citizens. That's why the Negro Leagues existed."

The children were silent for a few moments, taking in what the Coach was telling them.

"But things are beginning to change, and you three

have a job to do," he said, before disappearing again.

"Yes, we do," said Jamie, her game face back on. "Hank Aaron arrives by train later today. What do you say we hide out here until he arrives at the ballpark?"

The children found a good hiding spot in the right-field bleachers. From there, they could clearly see a banner by the front gate that said "Welcome to Winston-Salem, North Carolina, Spring Training Home of the Indianapolis Clowns." They stayed out of sight while ballplayers arrived throughout the afternoon.

After several hours, Hank Aaron had still yet to arrive. All the other players and coaches were long gone. Jamie, MJ, and Juanito were just about to head back to the locker when they saw him. He came out of the dugout and strolled onto the diamond. He seemed a bit older than he did at Hartwell Field, but not much.

He was dressed in his street clothes and was holding a cardboard suitcase. He left it on the ground next to the first-base line. He walked out onto the field, kicked the dirt a bit by second base, and then walked over to dig in at the plate. He stared out at an imaginary pitcher and swung an imaginary bat—cross-handed.

He was all alone in the ballpark, except for the children.

"Let's go," said Jamie.

The three kids made their way from the right-field stands to behind the home team's dugout. There, they hopped the railing onto the field. Hank Aaron, still at the plate, saw them out of the corner of his eye. He rested his imaginary bat on his shoulder and turned to face them. They stopped a few feet away from home plate.

"I thought I was the only one here," he said.

After getting over the initial shock of having Hank Aaron—*the* Hank Aaron—speak to her, Jamie responded on behalf of her friends.

"We've been waiting for you, Mr. Aaron," she said nervously.

"Waiting for me? Why?" answered the ballplayer. "And please call me Henry."

"We want to help you out," said MJ excitedly.

"Help me out?" asked Hank. "With what?"

"We happened to notice that you hold the bat with your hands the wrong way," said Jamie. "We'd like to help you switch your hands so you can hit even more home runs."

"Yeah," chimed in Juanito. "We want to help you become the greatest home run hitter of all time."

"You do, huh?" said Henry, chuckling. "I don't think anyone will ever beat Babe Ruth's record. What is it—714 home runs?

"That's not to say I wouldn't mind coming in second, though."

He winked at the kids, who couldn't help but grin.

"Actually, I've pretty much trained myself all these years. Folks have tried to get me to fix my grip, but I've never felt the need to hold the bat any other way."

Jamie was certain this was the reason she and her friends had traveled back in time. So she began making her argument.

"None of the other players bat cross-handed, Henry,"

she said. "Doesn't that make you think you might at least try switching your hands?"

"I don't see why," Hank answered. "Most of them don't hit as well as I do."

The kids weren't really sure how to respond to that. After several seconds of silence, Jamie asked, "Haven't you wondered about it, though?"

"Well, yes, I have. And believe it or not, I thought about it very recently," Hank said. "The other night, I woke up with a strange feeling, like something was wrong. Can't really say what it was, but I haven't been hitting all that well since. Not one homer."

Jamie's eyes lit up. "It's a sign," she said. "We think you'll hit even better if you switch your hands. Why not give it a go? You've got nothing to lose, and we'd love to play some ball with you."

"Well, I'd be a fool not to take you up on your offer, then," Henry said, smiling. "I never turn down the opportunity to play more baseball."

MJ and Juanito ran back to the locker to get the

baseball gear. While Hank Aaron grabbed a bat and laced up his cleats, Jamie dragged a large bucket of baseballs from the dugout to just in front of the pitcher's mound.

"You know, Jamie, *I* have to be the first to pitch to Hank Aaron," said Juanito.

"Why you?" she asked angrily.

"Because I'm Juanito," he replied.

Jamie had heard this logic from her friend before. Juanito certainly did not suffer from a lack of confidence. In this instance, Jamie didn't have the energy to argue with him—especially not in front of a legend.

"Go ahead," she said, flipping Juanito one of the baseballs. "Just don't bean him."

She and MJ positioned themselves in the outfield, hoping to shag a few flies off the bat of Hammerin' Hank. It was all almost too good to be true.

"Let 'er rip!" yelled MJ from left-center field.

"Hit one out here!" shouted Jamie from right-center.

"OK, Henry," Juanito said. "Put your right hand

above your left and take a few swings. How's that feel?"

"Funny," said the ballplayer, "but I do seem to get a more complete follow-through."

"And with that follow-through, you'll get more power," said Juanito. "You should be hitting with your weight on your back foot, not your front." All of a sudden, he was a hitting instructor, thanks of course to the magic locker.

"I see what you mean," said Henry. "OK, pitch one in here."

Juanito threw a nice fat pitch, about belt high, right down the middle. But, due to his new-found abilities, it was harder than any pitch he had ever thrown—perfect for a young ballplayer trying to make it to the majors. Aaron swung. The ball rocketed off his bat and kept rising until it flew well over MJ's head and beyond the wall in left field.

The children stood in amazement.

Standing far back in the batter's box, Hank preferred a closed stance. He held the bat held high above his shoulder and away from his body. His timing was perfect, holding his swing until the last split second.

"Keep 'em coming," he said to Juanito.

For the next couple of hours, until the sun started to set, Juanito, MJ, and Jamie took turns pitching to Hank Aaron and chasing down his blasts. The children demonstrated tremendous skill on the diamond: MJ tracked down fly balls like an all-star outfielder while Jamie showed off a cannon for an arm and Juanito fielded line drives off the wall like a pro.

The Coach returned to watch from alongside the first-base line, but Hank couldn't see or hear him.

"See how strong young Henry's wrists are?" he said to the kids. "That's because he worked on an ice truck as a kid, hauling blocks of ice. Together with the new grip you showed him, those wrists help him launch shot after shot clear out of the park."

"Kids, I don't know how to thank you enough. But I think it's time we stopped," said an appreciative Hank Aaron. "It's almost dark."

Just then, a car skidded to a stop in the parking lot alongside the field. Out jumped the white man whom the children had seen earlier.

"Henry Louis Aaron!" the man in the suit yelled angrily, slamming the driver's side door closed. "Where have you been? I've been looking all over for you!"

"Uh-oh," said Henry. "It's Mr. Syd Pollock, the owner of the Clowns. Listen, I don't want you three to get in trouble for being here, so why don't you head on out. And thanks again for everything."

The kids took Hank's advice. Approaching the locker, they stopped to take one last look around.

"Can you believe it?" said MJ. "We actually played baseball with Hank Aaron."

"And we actually helped him," said Juanito.

"C'mon," said Jamie, looking over her shoulder. "Let's go home."

"I'm all for that," said MJ. "I know what you said about time standing still, but I just can't help but think my mom is waiting by the back door, ready to chew me out for being late."

The kids piled inside the locker. First, the door closed. Then, the locker began to shake and a glow of light came through the air vents at the top.

And then, just as suddenly, the locker stopped shaking, the light went away, and the door swung open.

4
THE SHOW

"**N**ow what?" said MJ in disbelief.

The children were not back in Jamie's garage. Not by a long shot.

"What's going on?" MJ asked, confused. "We helped Hank Aaron. We did our job. And that means we're supposed to be back home."

A tear started to form in the corner of his eye.

"I know, MJ," said Jamie. "I'm not sure why. But we'll find out, and everything will be fine."

"Yeah, bro," said Juanito. "Just think: When you're

not home, you don't have to clean your room and take out the trash. You've got to think positive, dude."

MJ cracked a small smile. His friends always had a way to make him feel better.

The three were, once again, in a ballpark. Only this time, it was different. Much different.

It was obviously not a community diamond like Hartwell Field. Nor was it a Negro League stadium on Tobacco Road. No, this one was a *ballpark*!

The locker had landed alongside several others just like it—this time, in a hallway just to the side of the main room in the clubhouse. As the three friends stepped out of the locker and into the light, they could barely comprehend their good fortune. Even MJ had to admit this was super cool.

The clubhouse was awesome, in every sense of the word. Everything was white, with red and blue trim. There were tables and chairs, a few couches, a couple of television sets, and even a refrigerator.

The players' "lockers" weren't even lockers at all,

but small closets with no doors, a small stool set in front of each one. Hanging inside were several uniforms. On the floor were several pairs of cleats and more than a few gloves. Perched on a shelf near the top, next to cans of shaving cream and deodorant, were a bunch of hats. Every one of them had a lower-case, cursive "a" on the front.

"Do you children know whose logo that is?" asked the Coach, who once again appeared from inside the locker.

The kids shook their heads from side to side. They had no idea.

"It's the logo of the Atlanta Braves, around the time of the early 1970s," said the Coach. "And you're in their clubhouse."

"I think I know what this means!" shouted an excited Juanito. "We're going to see Hank Aaron break Babe Ruth's record!"

"Either that, or we're going to *help* him break it," said Jamie, raising an eyebrow toward the Coach, who just smiled.

"How are we going to do that?" asked MJ.

The Coach only continued to grin as he walked back into the locker and disappeared. The kids would have to find that answer out on their own.

"Man, I hate when he just takes off like that," said Juanito.

"Well, we're here for a reason," said Jamie, "or else we would be back in the garage. Let's find out what it is."

The three friends started for the exit, but they only made it halfway across the room. Blocking their way was a pair of high-heeled shoes.

5
CHASING A GHOST

"What are you kids doing in here?" the woman asked. "Don't you know this is off-limits to fans?"

Jamie thought fast.

"My dad is one of the Braves," said Jamie.

"Is that right?" asked the woman. "Which one?"

Uh-oh, thought Jamie. Except for Hank Aaron, she didn't know any other Brave—especially one that played around the time Aaron broke Ruth's record. So Jamie tried to fake it the only way she knew how.

"The best one," she replied.

The lady laughed. "Good answer," she said. "Now, you'd better get to your seats if you want to watch batting practice. It's always fun to watch Hank belt them out, wouldn't you say?"

"Oh yeah," said Juanito, playing along. "We never miss that."

Just then, the lady dropped a number of envelopes on the ground. MJ bent down to help pick them up. He noticed that they were all addressed to Hank Aaron.

"All these letters are for Hank Aaron?" he asked. "Are they from his fans?"

"I doubt it," said the lady. "They're more likely from folks who don't want to see a black man break the record of a white man."

"You mean there are people who don't want Hammerin' Hank to become the home run king just because he's black?" asked MJ.

"America hasn't changed *that* much," the woman, who was white, responded. "There are still a lot of people who aren't happy about Hank Aaron breaking the

Babe's record. And that's sad, since he's the last Negro League player to make it to the major leagues," she said. "His breaking the record is a wonderful achievement for black ballplayers."

She took the letters that she had dropped back from MJ.

"In fact, I bet some of these letters are death threats," she added. "I should know. I'm Mr. Aaron's personal secretary, Carla Koplin. I've been opening these letters for him so he can focus on playing baseball.

"And you know what? Six out of every 10 of these say that he should either quit . . . *or else.*"

"Or else what?" asked a nervous MJ.

"Or else the people who wrote them will hurt him or his family," she said. "Maybe even kill him."

The three children were silent. You could hear a pin drop in the clubhouse.

Finally, Jamie spoke. "So Mr. Aaron doesn't know about the death threats?"

"Oh, he knows," said the woman. "He just hasn't

read any of his mail for quite a while, now that he's getting close to breaking the record. The FBI and I have been doing it for him."

"Wow," said Juanito. "We didn't know that."

"I think the threats began to strengthen his determination," the woman added. "Last year, at 39 years old, he started hitting homers at a faster pace than in any other year."

"Really?" asked MJ, with a smirk. "So, Ms. Koplin, do you think he's going to break the record?" Juanito looked at his friend and sneered.

"Young man," she said, looking MJ directly in the eye. "I wouldn't be surprised if he quits tonight and walks away with 713, *before* breaking the record."

So he was one home run short of tying the Babe!

"Mr. Aaron has been chasing the ghost of Babe Ruth for so long," Ms. Koplin continued. "He's tired of the threats and of talking to reporters. He's also annoyed that police officers have to follow him, and discouraged that so many people don't want to see him succeed—

even in 1973!"

A tear trickled down her face.

The kids didn't know what to say. Not only were they having trouble believing what Ms. Koplin was telling them, but they were finding it difficult to hold back the tears themselves.

"Henry has always been soft-spoken and calm, never one to let his emotions get the better of him, both on and off the field," Ms. Koplin added. "But now, I think this whole thing has just beaten him down."

6
FROM THE
MOUTHS OF BABES

"Would he really retire?" asked MJ.

"There's a real possibility," Ms. Koplin said. "The only thing keeping him going, aside from the values his parents taught him, is the pile of letters he's received from kids across the country.

"Those letters have been in support of him, encouraging him to break the record," said Ms. Koplin as she turned to leave. "I just wonder if it's enough."

As she left the clubhouse, the three friends from the future turned to face each other.

"Well, we're obviously not here to see Hank Aaron *hit* a home run," said Juanito, a bit disappointed.

"Yeah," said Jamie, "but we *are* here for a reason."

"I think we're supposed to write him a letter," said MJ.

"Just what I was thinking," said Jamie. "Let's get busy before the team comes in."

After putting their heads together (and writing two quick rough drafts), the kids came up with a letter. Jamie put it down on paper in her best handwriting.

Dear Henry,

We don't know if you remember us, but we're the three kids who helped you with your swing many years ago in Winston-Salem.

We're still big fans of yours, and we want to see you become baseball's all-time home run leader.

We know it hasn't been easy for

you. We realize a lot of people don't want you to pass Babe Ruth. But you deserve to break sports' most amazing record. Maybe if you do, you'll help the people who can only see black and white to see things more clearly.

They signed it *From three of your biggest fans.* Then they placed it on the stool in front of Hank's locker, climbed back into their own locker, and closed the door.

7
THE HOME RUN
THAT CHANGED AMERICA

"You've got to be kidding me," said MJ to no one in particular, as he poked his head out of the locker. Instead of seeing the familiar items of Jamie's garage, he saw what looked like a . . . janitor's closet.

There were mops, buckets, and brooms; cleaning products; and rolls and rolls of toilet paper.

"I can't believe it!" he added. "We're still not home yet. How can that be?"

"I don't know, MJ," said Jamie. "But, so far, every time we've traveled somewhere, it's been for a reason."

The kids exited the locker and opened the door of the custodian's closet. They could hear people, mostly children, talking in a room down the hall. As they made their way toward the voices, they saw a sign on the wall. It said "Boys & Girls Club of America."

"Hurry up," said a woman to the children. "The game is about to start."

The three time travelers noticed that the room, filled with about 30 kids and a handful of adults, was actually a large living room, with couches, chairs, and a small black and white television set. Everyone's eyes were glued to the TV, which was tuned to a baseball game.

"I've never seen you three here before, so welcome," said the woman. "We are always happy to have new folks join us. You picked a great night to visit, don't you think?"

The kids didn't know what she was talking about. But, as usual, Jamie figured out what to say.

"We sure did," she said smiling. "We wouldn't have missed this for the world."

"Why don't you take a seat on the couch over there," said the woman. "There's room for you to squeeze in."

The three friends made their way over to the couch and sat down.

"Do you think he'll do it tonight?" a young black man asked the three newcomers. "I really hope he does it tonight."

"So do I," said MJ, taking a page from Jamie's book. He didn't know what the young man was referring to, so he just agreed.

Just then, an older man stood up and addressed the group.

"I remember when Hank Aaron hit his first major leage home run all those years ago," he said. "I read about it in the local newspaper. Then, I got to hear him hit so many other home runs on the radio. Tonight, right here in Mobile, I hope to see him hit Number 715."

So they were back in Alabama—to *see* Hank Aaron break Babe Ruth's record.

"You don't want him to do it, do you?" another

child asked, this time addressing his question directly to Jamie. "You don't want to see a black man break the record of a white man."

Jamie looked at the kid. She was a bit surprised by the question, but quickly realized why he might ask. She remembered what Ms. Koplin had said about the feelings toward Aaron.

"I want nothing more than to see him break the record," said Jamie. "It's *his* time. And it's America's time. We're ready for it. And we want it to happen."

"Just the answer that child needed to hear," said the Coach, who had suddenly appeared behind the couch. "You did well, sports fans. Now, sit back and enjoy." Just as quickly as he had appeared, he was gone.

On the TV, a reporter was interviewing Hank Aaron. A crude graphic on the screen said it was a taped conversation, conducted during the off-season—not long after the children had left their letter for Hammerin' Hank in the Atlanta clubhouse.

"I have never lived a day in my life that someone

didn't remind me I'm black," Hank said."Because of the position I'm in, I hope I can inspire a few kids to be a success in life. I want to break Ruth's record as an example to children, especially black children.

"I dedicate this pursuit to the kids out there, because they're the ones who have shown me the greatest support."

Jamie, MJ, and Juanito smiled. Then they sat back to watch history unfold before their eyes—*again*. This time, though, it was on a black and white TV in the Boys & Girls Club of Mobile, Alabama, with a group of African American children who quickly became their friends.

Four nights earlier, Hank Aaron tied Ruth's record during his first at-bat of the 1974 season, against the Reds in Cincinnati. On this night, the Braves were hosting the Dodgers.

In the fourth inning, with Al Downing on the hill for Los Angeles, Aaron calmly walked to the plate. Chief Noc-a-Homa, the Brave's mascot, was perched in front of his teepee. He was waiting along with everyone else—both white and African American fans all across the country—for something magical to occur. No one had to wait long.

Downing's first pitch to Aaron was in the dirt, which prompted the crowd to boo. His second pitch was a fastball, low and down the middle. Hank snapped his wrists and followed through.

The ball rocketed just over the head of the shortstop. It kept rising until it sailed over the 385-foot sign in left field, landing in the Braves' bullpen, where it was caught by reliever Tom House. It was Hank's first swing of the game and his 715th career home run, the most ever.

The crowd cheered wildly. Some fans even joined Hank as he ran around the bases. Fireworks filled the sky. And the number "715" appeared on the scoreboard in lights.

The children at the Boys & Girls Club of Mobile yelled, cheered, and hugged each other into the following inning. They didn't need to watch any more of the game. They had seen what they tuned in for. But they stayed until the final out, not wanting the magic of the night to end.

Following the game, things quieted down in the TV room, as everyone wanted to hear what Henry Aaron had to say. One interview he gave that historic night made quite an impression on the kids, none more so than Jamie, MJ, and Juanito.

"I'm hoping someday that some kid, black or white, will hit more home runs than me," said Hank. "Whoever it is, I'll be pulling for them."

8
THERE'S NO PLACE LIKE . . . HOME?

"**N**ext stop, Jamie's garage," said MJ with a grin that went from ear to ear.

Jamie smiled back at her friend. "Well, we've earned it."

"Speak for yourselves," said Juanito. "I'm ready for another adventure. I don't want to go home yet. I'm having too much fun."

"This *is* great," said Jamie, nodding. "I can't believe how lucky we are to being doing this."

"It's an important honor indeed," said the Coach,